Ice Dream's Wish

A story for Children & Inner Children

second edition

NASRIN MOTTAHEDEH

ILLUSTRATED BY MEHRI DADGAR

Ice Dream's Wish was awarded First Place in the 2014 Purple Dragonfly Awards, charity/making a difference category, as well as receiving Honorable Mention for Illustrations. It also won the "Honoring Excellence" Gold Level Award in the May 2014 Mom's Choice awards, inspirational/motivational category. + 3 more on 2017

ISBN 978-0-9888829-1-1

Copyright © 2013-2015 by Nasrin Mottahedeh.
Edited by Burl Barer
Cover and Internal Design by Shahrzad Eshrati & Raya
Printed in USA

To Ameleia
for the twinkle in your eyes when listening to my stories

Nasrin

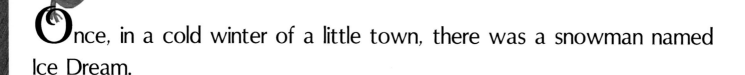

Once, in a cold winter of a little town, there was a snowman named Ice Dream.

He was white as cotton and cold as ice cream. He had a carrot nose, twigs for hands, a bright Valentine's scarf around his neck, and beads for buttons down his front.

Ice Dream looked very much like any other snowman, except that on the da᷉ he was made, the three children who made him decided to give him gifts to make him extra special.

They talked and talked, and even searched for special ideas on their compute᷉ They clicked and clicked until they found three gifts that would make him extra special:

A pair of sparkly marbles, a red rosebud, and a yellow apple.

The first child placed the pair of sparkly marbles above the snow-man's nose for eyes. The second child nestled the red rosebud in his chest for a heart. Finally, the third child placed the big yellow apple in his head for a brain.

These three special gifts gave Ice Dream a life of his own.

The snowman was happy when the three children were with him, playing outside and having fun.

But when they went to school every morning, he felt lonely and left out.

He wished that he could go find his three friends, but he was stuck in one spot. No matter how hard he tried, he couldn't move.

On one of those lonely days, as Ice Dream was missing the children, he thought to himself:

"I wish I could move just once in my life and go where I like. It's not fair! Everyone can move except for me. Every girl and boy, every dog and cat, this little brook, that red car, even that noisy airplane in the sky - they can all move, but I can't."

8

As Ice Dream watched the airplane etch a white trail across the sky, he saw some fluffy clouds. The clouds seemed to make different shapes. Some looked like little children playing with a ball, one looked like a tree holding snow on its branches and still, two other clouds were like teddy bears waiting to be hugged.

Then he saw a most amazing thing. Clouds came together, forming lovely angel wings, a beautiful crown, and a smiling face. This was more than just his imagination.

"Oh my goodness!" exclaimed Ice Dream, "It's a real angel!"

His excitement grew as the angel came closer and closer and began to speak:

"Hello Ice Dream!"

"Hi Miss Angel!" he said. "Who are you, and how do you know my name?"

"My name is Angel Cloud and I know all about you. I've come to make your wish come true. Are you ready to move around?"

9

Ice Dream looked at her in amazement and said:

"How did you know? Did I tell you about it? No I didn't! Did I call you for it? No I didn't! Did I write you asking for it? No I didn't! Did I even email you my wish? No I ..."

Angel Cloud interrupted him and said:

"Don't make it sound so difficult. Angels live in your heart and know of all you
wishes. In Angel World, we don't need to hear a wish, or receive a letter or a
phone call, text, or email." Then she joked: "Or be sent an instant message... c
you mention this one too?!"

Ice Dream felt embarrassed and said:

"I am sorry... I didn't know about your world."

The angel smiled kindly and said:

"Don't be sorry. You should never be ashamed of what you don't know
because that's how you learn new and exciting things every day. Now tell me
do you really want to move?"

The Snowman was so excited by hearing the word "move" that he yelled:
"Of course I do! Please! Please! Please! Please make me move!"

"All right, I will." Angel Cloud answered. "But you must know one thing: I will give you the power to move, but by the end of the day, there will be a big change in your life, a very big change."

The snowman asked curiously: "Can you tell me about this change?"

"No I can't. It's a surprise," answered Angel Cloud.

"At least give me a clue!" insisted Ice Dream.

"Very well. The only clue I will give you is that when you start moving, you will use your special gifts - your eyes, your heart, and your brain."

Eager to move, Ice Dream blurted out,

"It's okay, please just let me move!"

A second later, Ice Dream felt a strange sensation coming over him.

"What a feeling!" he exclaimed merrily. He moved to one side and then to the other side as he tried to balance.

"Wow!" he thought, "I can actually move!"

Ice Dream smiled to the angel, but suddenly, as he was gliding around, he stopped to ask an important question.

"Angel Cloud, what will the children think when they see me? Won't they be afraid of me?"

"Don't worry," said Angel Cloud. "I have already thought of that. You will be accepted as you are. Now go, and enjoy your wish."

The angel waved one wing goodbye and flew back into the sky.

13

The snowman thought for a moment.

"Hmm...where do I want to go?" He wanted to find the children's school to share his happiness with his three friends.

Following their footsteps in the snow, Ice Dream started to giggle like a child enjoying his first steps.

14

A few blocks down the road, he saw a hungry little bunny sitting by a tree. Unlike Ice Dream, he didn't look very happy at all. The snowman was so moved by the bunny's hunger that...

His marble eyes sparkled so kindly.
His rosebud heart was touched by love.
His apple brain shone with care.

So he walked up to the bunny and offered her his own nose, a juicy carrot. The bunny smiled, delighted by the snowman's kindness. She happily started chewing on the carrot.

Ice Dream went on his way, following the children's footprints in the snow. He was slipping, sliding, and having a wonderful time.

Soon he came across a young man who was helping an old woman in a car. Her car was stuck in the snow.

The snowman watched curiously. The car's tires kept swirling in the deep snow as the old woman steered. The young man and the old woman finally got the car moving again. The old woman thanked the young man for his help. Ice Dream was so moved by the young man's effort that...

His marble eyes sparkled so kindly.
His rosebud heart was touched by love.
His apple brain shone with care.

So Ice Dream offered the young man his red gloves. The gloves matched the young man's bare hands that were red from the bitter cold. The young man put the gloves on, shook Ice Dream's hand and gave him a wink.

17

Ice Dream happily continued on the path. Along the way, he saw a little girl in front of a toyshop asking her mother to buy her a box of beads so she could make a necklace for her favorite doll. Her mother explained that she would love to buy them for her, but she didn't have enough money. Although the little girl really wanted the beads, she looked up and said, "That's okay, Mommy, maybe later."

The snowman was so moved by the little girl's understanding that...

His marble eyes sparkled so kindly.
His rosebud heart was touched by love.
His apple brain shone with care.

So he looked down at his buttons, which were actually beads. He pulled them out, went up to the little girl, and handed her the beads. She jumped up and down and thanked him with a big hug.

The snowman kept going in his joyful journey, adding a skip and a hop to his step.

"Chirp...chirp...chirp..." A sad song came from two birds whose nest had been destroyed by the heavy snow. The snowman was so moved to see the birds' home broken that...

His marble eyes sparkled so kindly.
His rosebud heart was touched by love.
His apple brain shone with care.

So Ice Dream looked at his hands. He put them between broken branches on the tree so the birds could easily place twigs on them for a new nest. In a second, all the neighborhood birds came to help the two birds, each with a twig in its mouth.

"Chirp...chirp...chirp..." This time the two birds sounded very happy. It was a thank you song to the snowman and to all their helpful neighbors.

The snowman walked cheerfully on his way. He suddenly noticed a woman standing at a bus stop talking to a friend. She was pointing to a scarf full of little hearts that a young girl was wearing around her neck.

"I would love to get a scarf like that to give to my daughter as a Valentine's Day gift," she said.

"I have looked in all the shops, but I cannot find a scarf covered in Valentine hearts."

Because the snowman realized that he could help her...

His marble eyes sparkled so kindly.
His rosebud heart was touched by love.
His apple brain shone with care.

So Ice Dream came closer to the woman and asked her to take off the very similar scarf he had around his snowy neck. The woman, in joyful surprise, took the scarf, waved to her friend, and ran to the bus that had just arrived. On the foggy bus window, she wrote THANK YOU!!

At long last, Ice Dream followed the children's footprints all the way to the schoolyard.

He saw a bunch of happy children playing with snowballs. They were so busy running, dodging, sliding, laughing, and throwing snowballs everywhere that they did not notice Ice Dream.

The snowman was caught in the flying snow. By the time the fun was over, Ice Dream looked nothing like himself.

$\mathcal{A}$s the children were gathering their things to go home, the boy who had given the snowman his eyes suddenly saw the marble eyes lying in the snow. He picked them up and noticed a brighter sparkle to them. The boy did not know the marble eyes were glowing differently because of the kindness they had experienced that day.

The girl, who had given the snowman the rosebud heart, found it a few steps away and noticed how it had changed. She did not know that all the love Ice Dream had felt during that day had filled his heart, helping it blossom into a perfect rose.

The third child who had given the snowman his brain reached for the apple that had rolled far from where they were playing. She didn't know that caring for others had made the apple shine.

The three children looked at each other in wonder.

They understood that something strange and wonderful had happened to their snowman. What amazed them more than finding him at school was how spectacular their simple gifts had become. They were so moved by all the changes that...

Their surprised eyes sparkled so kindly.
Their beating hearts were touched by love.
And their smart brains shone with care.

The three friends took one look at each other and knew exactly what they wanted to do.

Before school the next morning, with fresh snow from the last night's snowfall, they got together to make their snowman once again. To their surprise, a bunny, two birds, a little girl, a young man, and a lady who got off the bus all came over to help.

After giving him a new carrot for his nose, a pair of branches for his hands, a set of new red gloves and a bunch of colorful beads, it was time to give him the same special gifts they had given him before:

The first child placed the pair of sparkling marbles above the snowman's nose as eyes. The second child nestled the perfect rose in his chest as a heart, and the third child gave the snowman the shining yellow apple as a brain.

Once they wrapped a brand new scarf covered in little hearts around his neck, they stepped back and looked at their snowman. They all saw that even though he looked the same, there was something wonderfully different about him.

What made him so extra lovable had nothing to do with his nose or his clothes. Kindness, love, and helping others – these are special gifts that make anyone more lovable, even a snowman.

A few minutes later, the kids were leaving to go to school. When they turned around to wave goodbye to Ice Dream, they noticed that the snowman was looking up to the sky. Curious to know what Ice Dream was looking at, they looked up too. Their snowman was smiling at the only piece of cloud in the whole blue sky, a cloud shaped very much like an angel!

30

Note

e

Nasrin Mottahedeh, Author

Mehri Dadgar, Illustrator

Burl Barer, Editor

Nasrin Mottahedeh is a native of Tehran, Iran. After receiving her Bachelor of Arts degree in psychology from The University of Tehran, she continued her education in journalism in the United Kingdom. Upon her return to Iran, she finished her education in broadcasting and pursued writing.

Alongside writing articles for children and adults in various magazines and newspapers, Nasrin began to write and produce content for Iranian National TV, including family shows and literature programs. Her show "A trip from spring to paradise" was nominated and won the award for best TV show in 1976.

After coming to America with her family, she founded and was the editor-in-chief of ZAN magazine, a publication for the Iranian community. ZAN magazine was very well-loved, especially among Iranian writers and women.

Nasrin is extremely creative with a brilliant sense of humor that reflects well in her work. Ice Dream's Wish is her first children's book and she currently is working on her next one.

Mehri Dadgar was born and raised in Iran.
She first attended art school at Art University in Tehran.
Later immigrating to the United States, Mehri earned her Master's Degrees in Art from California State University, Northridge.
She went on to receive an MFA degree in Studio Art from California State University, Long Beach.
Mehri has had a solo exhibition of her paintings at Cambridge University in England, as well as being selected for the Annual New American Paintings expo.
A prolific artist, Mehri is also involved in film, including making a Cinéma vérité documentary on the children of orphanages in Mexico and a Slice-of-Life about the workers and patrons of a Southern California car wash. Mehri's film, In the Grave, won a Gold Remi at the 40th Annual Houston International Film Festival.

Burl Barer is an Edgar Award win
American author, a literary histor
and a radio personality.
Burl began his broadcast career i
Pacific Northwest, and went on t
write and produce national radio
commercials for touring perform
including Frank Sinatra and Bob
Dylan, as well as launching sever
radio stations.
In addition to authoring many bo
on true crime and popular cultur
is considered an expert on the w
of Leslie Charteris, especially the
character Simon Templar. In 1997
Burl had two novels published, T
Saint, a novelization of the screen
for the film of the same name sta
Val Kilmer, and Capture the Saint
Burl has appeared on several
Investigation Discovery televisior
shows, and in 2013, served as a
consultant to the pilot series, "Th
Saint."

Ice Dream looked very much like any other snowman, except that on the day was made, the three children who made him decided to give him gifts to make him extra special...

"Ice Dream's Wish is a very attractive s not only for children of four or five, but also for old men of 94 and 95."
-Professor Ehsan Yarshater, founder and director The Center for Iranian Studies at Columbia University

"...a story about caring, about wishir about sharing and about the rewards kindness, It is a complete winner!"
-Grady Harp, Art and Poetry Reviewer for POETS and ARTISTS magazine

"An absolutely lovely and uplifting children's book with a truly positive and moral lesson."
-Burl Barer, author, literary historian and radio ho

"Ice Dream's Wish is engaging, empathetic, enchanting, and instructive
-H. Fayyad, Film Director and Critic

www.icedreamswish.com